CHRISTMAS AT HOME

J. ROD

Christmas at home
J. Rod

First edition December 2020
First published Mexico City, December 2020

"This story is dedicated to all my family, friends, acquaintances and people who lost the battle in the current war against the pandemic, directly or indirectly. To all of them who took care of themselves, took care of us and stayed at home as responsible citizens and friends. My respect for them, forever."

INDEX

CHRISTMAS AT HOME

J. ROD

Prologue

May 27, 2027.

Southern afternoons on the Gulf of Mexico coast are calm, especially when the sun goes down and the ocean breeze begins to cool. They are like a balm for the body of each person, after an intense day exposed to heat. It is as if the theory of the movement of molecules, that one that at a higher speed with the increase in temperature also applies to people, and when feeling the heat decrease, everything becomes peaceful. More in spring, close to summer, some say that May is the hottest month at this latitude.

That day the afternoon was different. The bustle in the city was unusual and strident. The streets of each neighborhood looked crowded, rivers of people walked through all of them, the alleys as if it were a carnival day three months ago, however, the noise was greater, perhaps by drums everywhere rumbling and raising the decibels of the celebration.

Juanito had grown into a tall, stocky college boy. He lived in that old house where he lived with his father until the day he left him to face his fate. His mother had passed away a year before from a terminal illness. He did not understand the reason for so much hubbub on any given Thursday in the city where he had always lived. He was just coming home from an extensive Econometrics class, part of the fourth—semester curriculum of his promising career as an economist. He opened the refrigerator and took out some mate herb to make it as a tea. He did it every afternoon while watching the sunset over the sea in the distance.

His Uruguayan and Argentine friends hated that action. For them, the mate herb had to be served in their style, with its leather cup and light bulb, but doing it in another way seemed an insult to their traditions. For him it was just not complicating himself to drink that flavor that reminded him of the last trip with his father to the ice, to the Perito Moreno Glacier on Argentino Lake, where he tasted that customary hot drink from Las Pampas for the first time. Sometimes you could even perceive a cold sensation when you feel that taste in your pupils, despite the high temperature of the Veracruz coast in the Gulf of Mexico in the middle of spring. Perhaps caused by that refreshing breeze as the temperature drops when the sun goes down. He sat on a hammock in the garden. The afternoon was beginning to fall, the rays of the sun flashed with less intensity on the waves, whose characteristic sound when breaking with the stones was overshadowed by the unknown celebration. Not even the wind waving the flags of the palm trees could be heard with so much enthusiasm wasted on the sidewalks.

Despite being a young man not used to partying or celebrating a celebration in the city, curiosity made him go out the front door and he stayed there in the immense porch, but worn by the years, listening to songs that were not made to him. Feeling and seeing the fireworks, barely perceptible through the still existing clearing in the beautiful blue sky that afternoon.
An old—fashioned Japanese—made taxi pulled up just outside his house, where he stared blankly at the popular celebration, trying to guess why. It was strange to see a person driving a public transport car. Most were conducted by remote control, which generated more safety for the crew and efficiency for the company to which they belonged, by being able to remotely control routes, and assisted by technology to minimize arrival times.

He was an old man with a disheveled and dirty white beard, but very well dressed. It caused great anxiety in Juanito who turned his gaze from the festive crowd to the taxi, feeling disturbed by the presence of someone unknown at the door of his house. The alarming rates of insecurity in the city had not decreased in a decade, despite multiple government strategies to bring it down.

For that reason, it was difficult for him to direct his timid gaze to the driver's. He was shaking with fear. He had never felt that tension in his veins. It was as if ice had been put in each of his arteries, making his skin crawl with terror.

— Hey kid! Are you Juanito? — Said the old taxi driver with a deep and hoarse voice that horrified Juanito, now not only because of the sound, but also because he called him by his own name and because of the hidden interest of an unknown adult to find him. He did not know whether to respond instantly or pretend not to know who that subject was looking for. Adrenaline quickened his pulse, and his shaking hand dropped the teacup held in his right hand.

The old driver put his right hand on top of the compartment located between his seat and the passenger seat. He opened it slowly. Juanito imagined the worst: a firearm or some bad sign would extract the old man from that loophole.

— Easy, boy — said the old man, — I'm not going to hurt you.

Every second that advanced the clarity began to disappear and the night became more and more evident. The taxi driver took a cardboard box from inside the compartment.

— I was commissioned to deliver this package to you.

Juanito's mind began to imagine who could have sent him that package. He had almost no relatives and saw his friends every day at the university.

— I haven't bought anything by parcel. — He managed to answer.

The old man just smiled and that gave the young university student a bit of reassurance so that he could normalize his breathing, but he continued to feel curious.

— It is an order made approximately seven years ago by a guy very similar to you, and since we Veracruz people comply with our agreements, I am here to give it to you.

Juanito still didn't understand. He thought it was a joke from someone he knew, perhaps related to the celebration of that day in the city.

— I have no idea, but if it has no addressee, I will not receive it. - he answered and walked towards the door of his house to leave.

But the old man yelled at him:

— Do you know Juan Martín Zelaya Torruco?

That boy's eyes filled with tears profusely, and in the next instant he wouldn't stop crying and sobbing. As he could, he approached the window of the vehicle and quickly took the cardboard box. He could barely articulate a couple of broken words.

— Thank you very much!

And he ran to the entrance to enter the interior of his home and review the contents of that package expected for seven long years.

1

The inopportune moment

Just the day that I woke up to the intense rays of dawn burning my pupils, I discovered the greatest joy of my life in the half—sleeping smile of my first—born son leaning on my right shoulder.

The world turned loudly. It was faster than 24 hours of translation, more spontaneous than a shooting star. It was an abrupt, instantaneous movement. But a couple of words heard that same day transformed my happiness into anguish.

My head just clearing began to process every moment around me. At what point did he grow so big that I couldn't bear his long and heavy thigh leaning on my abdomen while he continued to sleep on his side facing me. At which point he stopped being a baby, my baby, to become a teenager the size of an adult, about to exceed my average height. However, his smile and face still seemed to me that of a baby, whom I had to protect from the voracious world and make every moment of his life happy. Those resolutions crossed my mind from the moment I heard him cry through that foggy glass, where his mother gave birth to him on February 23, 2008. I felt that time had not passed, not a fraction of a second, but for my misfortune did happen. He was almost a teenager and yet I kept seeing a baby that made me pause as I stood admiring him.

The alarm rang. It was six o'clock in the morning. I had plenty of time to get up, put on my running shoes, and feel the ocean breeze while doing my 25—minute daily cardio routine. I like to shower with cold water to feel the contrast with my accelerated body touching every part of my body, with the tingling produced by running free of that transparent liquid and its force of gravity. I enjoy taking the vitamins recommended by the doctor for my 50 years, and also drinking a cup of steaming coffee, relaxed, while watching the sunrise through the window enjoying the aroma of the morning with coffee. I usually have a light breakfast with fruits and yogurt, and accompany it with toasted bread with butter, my favorite combination. I love to dress slowly by knotting my tie calmly to have the exact measurement my father taught me since my teens. The tip of the tie just touching the belt. The alarm sounded again, and without making the slightest attempt to stop it, I glanced sleepily at the clock again. I turned to my right once more, saw his face and decided to immediately slap it off.

A minute later I imagined my commute to work in a comfortable and safe vehicle, with the pleasant climate of the air conditioning, despite the summer heat, without breaking a sweat, still with my jacket and tie covering me, and drinking a little more coffee on the way, enjoying its unique steaming aroma in my reinforced steel mug that kept my drink warm until noon. And thanking God for the privilege of having the way to transport myself, but above all having the legs to step on the pedals, firm hands to hold the wheel and the knowledge to do it routinely and safely. Observing this ritual in my mind, I quickly counted the time to run, shower and dress to get to work at 8:30 am. I calculated the time I could sacrifice and set the alarm 45 minutes after normal time so I could stare at that innocent face longer. It looked like a photo of me, from when I was a child. The tranquility of watching over his sleep filled me with peace. To be there feeling the weight of his grown body was a happiness incomparable with any success, reward, gift or experience. I hugged him tightly without waking him up and realized that he loved smelling the floral scent of his hair from some children's shampoo.

My body asked me to exercise like every day to feel that sensation of freshness sweating toxins and feel how each part accelerated and filled life with each trot on the soft sand of the beach, inhaling the fresh breeze. However, that pleasant sensation of seeing the fragility of a being in my gut, called me not to detach myself from there, until the moment when there was no more time available to get to work on time, and so I decided to do it, to contemplate each gesture over and over again, drawing the same or new conclusions. He was identical to me, even in the prominent cheeks, or those eyebrows inherited from my paternal family that form almost a single one because they even slightly cover the brow bones, although in a smaller but perceptible portion. His straight nose, his abundant shaved hair unlike mine that one day was like that, but the ravages of time reduced my hair, perhaps due to heredity, poor diet, illness or all three together.

The morning was nice. In a city where the temperature never drops below 18 degrees, sunrise at 21 was akin to experiencing a freezing winter. For moments I kissed his forehead, taking care not to wake him up. Time passed and at that moment I remembered the sensations experienced with him at different times in my life, which I had described as the most beautiful. Like when I traveled through the majestic mangroves of Cartagena under a persistent rain drinking a Colombian beer, delving into narrow paths away from civilization until I reached a spectacular, virgin beach, where I could rest in a hammock, while I was delighted with gastronomic delights, or when I chopped ice from that endless glacier known as Perito Moreno, with my hands asleep from the cold of the ice and the exterior of just two degrees Celsius. I brought with me a glass where I added the ice and a little Single Malt The Balvenie 25 year old whiskey, which I had just to toast feeling the icy breeze on my reddened and parched face, like that of my eternal companion. The famous 2020 drink, 2000 years of the glacier and 20 of the whiskey, although my favorite was 25 years. Feeling that hot taste of liquor in my taste buds contrasting with the old ice and the freezing weather outside, made my skin crawl. The colors that form with frozen ice are impressive. It is a range of blues, the widest observed. That feeling of being there relaxed as if one could stop time and have the world completely at one's feet, after having traveled hours and thousands of kilometers to see those places.

I also remember when I reached the top of the Chinese wall exhausted with my cheeks anesthetized by the intense cold that it is at the highest part of that historic road. He was also next to me. His cheeks were red. Or contemplate the Cathedral of Florence with that never—before—seen combination of three colors: green, white and pink. While uncorking a bottle of wine and had his counterpart accompany me on that trip, perhaps the most beautiful of my life, my father. Or when I enjoyed the view of the Swiss Alps with a delicious and frothy hot chocolate lost in the immensity of those snow—covered mountains, feeling an incomparable happiness when communicating that feeling of freedom and greatness of having the privilege of being there before a designed landscape by God, unique and unrepeatable.

I realized that those spectacular sensations were compared every morning of confinement, having Juanito lying on my arm sleeping in front of me, under three layers of sheets due to the intense cold of the air conditioning at low temperature as he liked to face the hot weather southern nights of Veracruz.

I watched his angelic gestures, feeling proud to be raising a child to be a good man in the future. At that moment I was wondering if my son would be a good man like I thought he was or much better than me. This translucent judgment of my goal to achieve overwhelmed me as I watched him settle and move frequently on my sleepy shoulder, perhaps dreaming of some childhood fantasy.

The prolonged confinement in our country due to the poor implementation of a strategy to face the pandemic made me spend more time than expected working at home, taking care of the health of the only person I loved in the world, my son. Thanks to these events, I realized that I did not need to travel kilometers, or exotic drinks, or see unique landscapes to experience the same feelings of infinite happiness. Maybe it was too late, maybe not, if every minute with him was like 20 years of my life of happiness.

I remember how I wished that by the time Christmas arrived we could travel and travel around the world together, as we had not done for a couple of years due to overwork.

So many dreams, so many hopes, but the least expected day arrived, the least opportune moment, that moment for which we are never prepared.

2

Bad news

That morning I left Juanito with my mother, his favorite grandmother, to attend the pending appointment with the doctor after having done all kinds of studies in the week. He hoped that this mild headache every morning would not go beyond a decompensation, a migraine or perhaps a discomfort caused by the excess salt that I ate with food. However, as I entered Dr. Vernoulli's impeccably white office, his contrite face anticipated unpleasant news at first. So, bluntly and without much medical jargon, I got to the point. If it was something not serious, then what did it matter to know and return immediately to my mother's house for Juanito and take him to eat pizza in front of the sea,and if it was something to be alarmed, then at once take that difficult step and begin to gain every second of my few available.

— How serious is it, doctor?

I had known the doctor for more than 40 years. He had cared for my mother and also my father before he passed away. So we were always direct, as well as great friends. His nervous hand was constantly hitting the desk. He frowned in a way never seen before and my skin began to feel an intense cold starting from my almost numb feet. The uncertainty gnawed at me.

— Very serious, Martín. — he told me, dry, brooding.

His imprecise words worried me more. Not telling me clearly what was happening, it was a sign of the worst news, but it could also be a curable disease or one that could be controlled for years, to be able to accompany Juanito to enter the university hand in hand with me on his first day. I could also only last a few months to do the most important things in my life.

I thought it would last for weeks or days, like a Russian roulette that I obviously didn't want to play.

I watched how the lamp that illuminates the room began to bother my view, my body felt heavy. I never thought I would find myself in a situation like this, especially when you have discovered happiness in your son's smile.

With a choked voice and my skin sweating, I could barely question:

— How much time do I have?

Although it was the right question not to waste any more time, I kept wishing in my mind over and over again that it was the wrong question. That the most serious thing was the need for a dangerous transplant or a chronic disease with which I could survive, even with a lower quality of life and more with that gift of God discovered in quarantine, was just the moment when I most wanted to live.

I always hated doctors' offices. Normally, I attended them for routine tests or tests. I hated them since I was a child when they operated on me for appendicitis and I was for months without being able to go out to play with my friends due to later complications. I knew it was a gamble to frequent those places. Anything could happen, like this day.

— A couple of months, Martín, I'm very sorry. — was the answer that hit me like a bucket of cold water. - You are in the terminal stage of pancreatic cancer.

The nightmare had become a reality, revealed by Dr. Vernouli's cold words. I know that this situation hurt him too, although the relationship was strictly professional, our passion for football made us coincide a couple of times on a trip to see the San Francisco 49ers. Their little children played with my Juanito for many years in the soccer academy of the city. Since then we were no longer just a doctor and his patient, but two great friends with similar tastes. You could almost even tell that his eyes sparkled for a few minutes trying to avoid crying. There was only one question left to ask before retiring to take advantage of that couple of months, every moment, with my son.

— Is there something to do? — I asked and his response was transfigured into seeing him shrug slowly and shake his head from left to right. The silence was sepulchral. — Well, in that case, I would like to see if it is possible to fulfill a wish that I have always had at this moment — I stammered.

— Yes, tell me Martin. — the doctor responded me.

— I have always wanted to contribute something to humanity when I am gone. — I told him as I sat, already resigned to my departure, in the cold white leather seat of his office. — I have seldom done anything for my fellow men. — I have been absorbed in work trying to have many professional and financial successes, and that is why I wanted to ask you if it would be possible to donate my organs when they are no longer there so that my life has some use.

I could barely speak and as much as I tried to avoid it, streams of tears ran down my cheeks, just thinking about birthdays, Christmas, summers, soccer games and more moments when I would no longer enjoy being with him. The smell of alcohol from hospitals made me nauseous. I just wanted to hear from my doctor friend the possibility of my request and run away.

— It would be necessary to carry out an assessment of which organs have not been affected by cancer or by any other health condition in your body. In fact, the ideal would be that when you can still travel, do all these studies and immediately proceed to stay hospitalized to wait, while the doctors carry out the studies and try to better conserve the possible organs to donate.

— Will I make it to Christmas? — I blurted out almost naturally. I knew that even though I was the goner, Vernoulli wasn't having a good time with my doubts and woes, either.

— It's complicated, but hopefully with pain treatment we can do it.

He understood what I meant. I wanted to be able to enjoy that intimate and familiar moment and then leave and not return home.

— Come on, doctor, let's try it. — I want to spend, even one last Christmas with Juanito — I proposed.

— I'll do my best, — the doctor told me, — but you must promise me that you will take good care of yourself from now on. No alcohol, tobacco, junk food, excesses, and above all take all the precautions against the coronavirus pandemic, because a contagion for you would be lethal.

— I will, doc, whatever it takes to get to December 25th. October is almost over, so if your predictions are good I will have plenty of time.

I left the office as when my ears get congested by a cold, without listening clearly, without being able to focus my gaze on something, with my eyes wet from pain. Standing at the door of the clinic, I did not know what direction to take.

What would you do if for a moment you found out that you could practically die in the next few hours?

3

Mothers love

I was still groggy, walking towards my vehicle, and grabbed my cell phone with my hands still shaking. For every human being there is only something that alleviates any evil, so I marked the only infallible antidote for any pain: my mother.

— Hello son, how are you? How did it go with the doctor?

— Mom!

— Yes, tell me Martín, what's up.

— I love you very much — my eyes were flooded with tears and I couldn't continue: my voice was cut off and I didn't pronounce any word well.

— Son, what's up.

I hung up the call and even though she dialed me several times, I didn't answer; I preferred to go to her house and tell her personally.

My mother saw me crying when I entered her house; so she took me to the home study and sat in my father's work chair. I wanted to prevent Juanito from noticing my state while playing video games in what used to be my room. However, just being in that place, where many times my father took me to play while he worked late to feel close, made me feel a little more comfortable. The scent of that cedar wood, the fine leather of his study, and the dim light coming through the skylight, were soothing to me at the time.

My mind was recalling that little boy playing with miniature racing cars all over the soft brown carpet. The air conditioning at a low temperature as my father liked, who always made me wear a sweater to avoid catching a cold, shouting when simulating the noise of the engines and my father lovingly laughing and telling me while covering the telephone receiver with his hand so that not make such loud sounds. One day he just told me: "Son, life is a journey and death is a destination," and went back to work at the brown marble desk.

That angelic voice interrupted that involuntary journey of my mind by being in that place and cut a little bit of crying.

— What's going on Son.

— Mother, although we have never gotten along so well, I want to tell you that I love you.

— I know, son, - she said as she got up from the chair quickly to hug me, while I sobbed a little.

— You think my dad knew it, that like you was the main thing for me.

— Those were just the last words of your father before leaving in the hospital bed. "Do you think Martín knows what is most important to me". I answered him without hesitation that yes, that "for him you are his maximum", and he closed his eyes calmly.

— I don't want to leave Juanito. — I said, sobbing in her arms.

— Why are you leaving him? Does Estela want him to live with her?

For several minutes I did not stop sobbing, until I gradually calmed my chest and felt calmer to be able to talk without stopping.

— The doctor told me that I only have two months to live.

My mother's eyes began to shine and she hugged me very tight.

— Don't worry, son, I'll be with you always.

— I know, Mom, but I don't know if I can bear saying goodbye to Juanito.

We went into the room, where Juanito played unconcerned with anything mundane.

— Dad, it's good that you arrived. Play this game with me.

There are moments in life that I have been able to endure crying, no matter how uncontrollable it may be. I remember for example when Estela told me that she would leave the house with suitcases in hand. I felt like dying, but I couldn't vanish for Juanito. That is why I endured like a warrior the urge to cry in front of her, for not showing her the undeserved and irreversible damage she was doing to me, but also so that Juanito would not realize what was happening.

Juanito was at that time an innocent four—year—old boy playing with a stuffed toy in the living room of the house, watching his mother leave without knowing that it was forever. I also held back the urge to cry when my father died because everyone was devastated and my older uncle, told me I should be strong for the family and be the leader, the guide we need.

But this moment far exceeded any pain in the world, I had to make a mandatory stopover before he could talk to him.

— Of course I will, son, just let me pour some coffee in Grandma's kitchen. You like a little chocolate— I could barely express this last word without losing my voice and I immediately left the room towards the kitchen with Grandma behind me.

My mother made the coffee and chocolate. We both drank a little before going to the bedroom.

— Try to calm down, son. Juanito can't see you weak. For him you are his hero and heroes are not destroyed by anything or anyone.

She was right, I should draw strength from where he could. I drank a cup of hot coffee without stopping and without sugar to feel that bitter and stimulating taste travels my throat, burning it a little, and that pain distracted a little from the greater pain that afflicted me. In fractions of seconds the calming effect of the drink numbed my senses. I took several deep breaths and imagined scenarios that would cause me joy, past trips with Juanito to try to reverse the pain and be able to calm my tears at least as soon as we got home.

We enter the room again

— Son, we can play at our house. Your grandmother must be tired.

He made a disapproving face for leaving the game he was playing excitedly unfinished. I hugged him and we said goodbye to Grandma.

We got home and the first thing he did was turn on his video game console, sit on the carpet leaning his back on the couch and challenge me to play the soccer game called FIFA. As always, he chose Barcelona and I obviously chose the archrival and the best team in the world, Real Madrid. His smile, while excitedly handling the control, calmed my pain in a surprising way.

Suddenly seeing him take that control into his little hands and smiling every time he scored on my goal was a balm for my life.

— Son, I have something to tell you.

— What dad?

He turned around with his usual face of surprise and despair for interrupting the current game. I didn't have the courage to tell him about my illness. It was such a perfect moment and there were plenty of sad explanations. I better think about the next day, what would the first day of the last less than a hundred days of life that I have left?

4

To hell with quarantine

Surprisingly, I woke up before the strident sound of the daily alarm of my alarm clock, bored perhaps of waking up to the same old song, "Shark smile", by Big Thief, which reminded me of the deep gaze of Juanito's mother.

Perhaps my son's snoring was a prettier song than the alarm set to end my break, or maybe my mind knew of the little time available to me and had unconsciously proposed to make the most of the most insignificant second of my life, next to my firstborn.

The math class that Friday, October 30, started at 7:00 a.m. The teacher, as usually those who teach this subject are, was very strict and demanding. That is why when it was time to take it, Juanito would wake up fifteen minutes earlier than usual. He was seconds away from the deadline and I began to move him from side to side to wake him up. If it was always an ordeal for me to wake up early to go to school, it was even worse to have to cut off the sleep of the person I loved most in the world, and seeing his fervent desire to rest for a couple of minutes was even more difficult, but I had to do it, and if I wanted to leave something valuable to my son, it was precisely that, the sense of responsibility. When I was shaking him and yelling at him to get up, I was again aware of the immensity of his size.

How could the cuddly baby of a decade ago have turned into a sturdy oak, full of life. A snapshot of him in my mind, dressed in a dark gown and gold cap, graduating from college, flashing the endless smile of success on his face, was enough to neglect my daily homework.

A split second changed my perspective and my decision making. I quickly went downstairs to the kitchen and pulled out a couple of alfajores stored in the refrigerator from our trip to Argentina last year. I started making tea and in the blender I made some milk chocolate with lots of ice. I arranged the alfajores and the drinks on the tray, and I put it up, leaving it on Juanito's bedside table. I turned on the television without sound so that it would not wake up and I chose a beautiful image of the glacier with the contrasts of the purity of white and that brilliant blue of the sky in the sea. I turned on the music player to play the tango that we liked so much: "por una cabeza", and turned up the volume.

— It's time to get up, Juanito, — I said, and he, writhing on the bed, got up little by little until he was standing up, all drowsy.

— Can I come down for a minute for something to eat, Dad? — He told me. His voice dragged the words from the wakefulness of a previous day watching cartoons.

— Why are you going down? If breakfast is already served — I questioned, pointing my finger at him. He hadn't noticed the tray served next to him.

— Thanks Dad. Today it's math. At least I will connect with the satisfaction of the chocolate, — Juanito said with a smile on his face.

— Today you will not enter class, son — I said and his eyes finished opening completely and his staggering walk was corrected. The very idea of not having class wiped the dream from his mind instantly.

— So what shall we do, Dad? — He expressed. His voice was infectious with enthusiasm. I stared at him, smiling, excited to see his surprised face.

— Forget about classes for today. It is time to travel and vacation.

For each word I said, his emotion grew until he said the last ones where his face became annoyed and he felt disappointed.

— Dad, stop joking with me.

Juanito threw the pillow to the side of the bed and began to put on the shirt of the Benavente School uniform. I went to the blind and began slowly to close it until there was no gap that allowed the light to enter. I turned on the air conditioning, which I had just turned off, to save electricity, when I woke up. I pressed the button to set the temperature to the minimum, as well as the fan speed to the maximum.

— Dad, what are you doing? I can't put my uniform on in such low light.

— I told you it was time to travel, son.

— Dad, stop joking, that you don't have to take online classes and feel sad because my classmates are not close to me.

Juanito was beginning to get annoyed by what he thought were my jokes.

— I'm not kidding, son, today you will not connect to your classes. We will go on a trip, you and I, like in good times.

By repeating it one more time, Juanito changed his face to one of less annoyance, although he still hadn't finished trusting my proposal one hundred percent, and that's why I continued with the plan by taking a suitcase out of the closet.

— Dad, are you serious? But at this time almost all destinations are closed due to the pandemic. Let's see, tell me, where will we go? - He said to me now with a clear emotion on his face.

— On the ice. Remember when you said that to me, 'Dad I want to go to the ice'.

— Aha, yes, we will go to Argentina right now that it is in the middle of autumn and the pandemic is at its greatest risk.

— Exactly! We will go to the coldest place on the continent right now. We will return to Calafate, Argentina, to see the Perito Moreno glacier once again.

Juanito continued dressing in his school uniform, reluctantly, not giving credit to what I said, but I stopped him and ordered him with my arm on his right shoulder to sit on his side of the bed.

— We're going to the ice, son, as you asked me that time when we visited Buenos Aires for work reasons. On that occasion you also missed class for a whole week to accompany me.

I put on the screen the videos we recorded of our trip to the ice, when he was just four years old. You could hear how the immense ice cracked and fell slowly into the water of the Argentine lake. With the blinds completely closed causing darkness and the freezing climate of the air conditioning, the feeling was as if we were there. Fortunately with that entire prepared environment he began to feel the emotion of the replica of that unforgettable moment in our lives.

— Do you remember that there is nothing more powerful in the universe than the human mind? - I told him as he beat his cheeks as he devoured the delicious gingerbread covered with chocolate and drank that smoothie that he liked so much.

— Yes, Dad, you've told me over and over again.

— Well, just let your imagination fly and stand there, at that point at the extreme where I, your father, shone with whiskey and ice from the glacier, that famous drink called 2020, for the two hundred years of aging of the ice and 20 of the liquor— I reminded him and Juanito looked at me smiling and leaned back on his bed staring at the screen, without blinking for a single moment.

So it remained for several minutes. I saw his excited face, and each time he covered himself with more sheets feeling the cold of that monumental ice.

— Will we ever go back there? — Juanito asked me looking into my eyes without blinking.

My cheeks began to tremble and my eyes, frozen by the weather, began to get moist and to feel my body freeze. Lying was not in my dictionary. I remembered the priest of the church of my town in my childhood, when he said that white lies did not exist. The dilemma was great, but my love for him was even greater. I hugged him tight.

— Yes, son, soon we will return to that place

5

No slopes

When I finished telling her everything that imploded me, she was speechless for a few minutes. I was drenched in tears. It was no wonder, we were inseparable since we were children and currently we work together. We made such a good team that we had formed a solid company, already with fifteen years of experience and great results.

I remember one afternoon at my grandparents' house playing baseball in the garage. We took as a bat a piece of wood from a piece of furniture that my grandfather built, and from a ball one that was harder than that officially used by professionals: they were stones from the gravel piled up in a corner of the garage used in the constructions made by the paternal grandfather. I remember how I laughed at her, so much so that she could not connect a single pitch no matter how slow it was. She knew that these teasing completely distracted her and put her in a very bad mood. I kept telling her that we'd better play something else because she would never hit the ball. I threw a rock at her with all my might so she couldn't even see it, but she mechanically moved the bat just to touch it, as baseball coaches say when you're a kid, just tap it. And yes, as soon as she saw my launch coming, I didn't even have time to do it, I just felt a strong blow and in an instant I had blood dripping from my mouth and I was chewing with my teeth two hard objects that I took out of my mouth. One was our supposed baseball and the other was my right incisor tooth. And while I couldn't believe it, now she was laughing out loud at her hitting.

There were all kinds of anecdotes in a lifetime of colleagues, accomplices, sometimes rivals for academic merits.

Sometimes also very emotional moments, such as, when I was past twenty, one day I was visiting my parents' house, reviewing their saved memories, she sent me a photo as evidence of a Christmas letter written by me, when I was just eleven years old and where, among all my requests, at the end I asked for a rattle for my little sister, or when I attended her university graduation, an important moment for the whole family, and even more so for me for feeling part of that achievement by having supported her on those sleepless nights with her thesis, drinking liters of coffee and beer on several occasions and wine. And her courage at seeing me unattainable in Scrabble games, where it took me a long time to find the perfect word that would give me the highest score against her claims for the delay in time.

Christmas together, lighting sparklers and making the traditional old man together with our cousins, a doll made of clothes stuffed with newspaper and explosives that we set on fire just at midnight to fire every year. However, these anecdotes were about to end in a couple of months and not by my own will, but by a series of unexpected events and which I could not control, but had to face in the most pleasant way as a good believer.

— Will you tell Juanito? — She told me when she managed to calm down a bit after completely drinking her coffee poured into the metal mug that I gave her at Christmas so that she could enjoy hier favorite hot drink for a longer time.

— No, he must not find out for the world. So please, I ask you to keep the secret — I asked him apparently to be the owner of the situation, although inside I felt devastated to see her pain for my departure. I felt calm because I had always been there to support her.

— What will you do this couple of months? — She asked me how, hinting that I was counting on her for everything I needed.

— I want to retire, I want to take advantage of until the last moment that I remain one hundred percent of my life to be with Juanito. That is all I want.

      — Of course, you know that you shouldn't worry about coming to work, forget about everything and just spend time with those who love you. - she said wishing to see us more often.

— Yes that's what I'll do. If you like, I can leave you signed the documents you want so as not to have problems when I'm not there.

— You don't have to worry about anything. I will solve any problem, do not worry — she expressed sure and giving me a little peace of mind for not leaving any pending that could affect the family business.

      — Thank you very much, sister, take good care of Juanito.

      — And his mom?

      — I'll talk to her next week to take care of him.

      — But she left him.

Then came a silence. My sister's resentment towards her for having abandoned us still did not stop. It was logical; whoever harmed her blood also harmed her.

      — She is her mother. And if she can't take care of it, Mom already said that she can take care of him like he was myself, like she did us.

— It's your decision. In any case, I will always be on the lookout for him. It will be very good. You will not be missing anything at any time. He and Diego may even go to college together, because they are the same age, and they have always been the closest cousins.

— Hopefully so.

We talked for a long time like when we spent a Christmas together for a long time, until it was time to say goodbye. It was a real sad moment. On the way back home, it was completely silent. I didn't want to hear anything; I just wanted to lengthen every second of every minute, every hour...

6

Irreparable losses

November 3, 2020

I was in shock: just the previous month I had received the news of the death of my best friend's brother, Marisol Talavera. She was not a very old person, and I always thought that, in a couple of days, she would be back home, but she never came back. I never imagined that ending in his life. From that day on, I decided to leave home as little as possible and do most of my work online. He wasn't many years older than me, so I decided that I shouldn't tempt fate and take more care of myself. The world seemed like a horrible science fiction movie, one of those apocalyptic ones, where the unexpected happens overnight, the same as a deranged mind.

The improbable, the unthinkable, would happen months later, according to the November 2019 newscasts that reported a strange event. In China, the appearance of a new virus that causes atypical pneumonia had been detected in those infected probably transmitted to humans by an animal: a bat or a pangolin. We Mexicans made memes, we laughed at that idea. When I first heard that information I believed that it would only affect the Far Eastern country. As the weeks passed, the news that initially took up a few minutes in the media began to cover more time until it reached special programs and live broadcasts.

Listening to the presidents of the three most populous countries in America: the United States, Brazil and Mexico, minimize the effects, caused neglect in the citizens, until each one began to feel the effects firsthand observing the losses of acquaintances. It was until then that we were able to understand how serious the problem was. In a war countries are destroyed, in a pandemic the loss is worldwide. And that day I felt a blow to my chest.

Until that moment, I already had several acquaintances who had fallen ill and died from the pandemic. I was left world when I received a message on my cell phone: the father of my lifelong friend, Guillermo Sánchez, was added to the death list. Just a week before, I saw his publications on his social networks enjoying the quarantine in his house. A few days later, he published that he had been infected. Shortly after he was admitted to the hospital due to lack of oxygen, the next day Memo told me they had intubated him and in the afternoon he was already receiving the fatal news.

Then a former student at the Isthmus American University passed away, where I teach classes on Saturdays. It was Osiris Ocejo, and hence the number of deaths continued to increase. In a single day, the parents of Eunice and Mirtza, two great friends, died. And the worst part was that there was not even a notion of how long the pandemic would last because the vaccine was still in the test phase and the world was helpless before a microscopic enemy. The uncertainty about the behavior of this disease was desperate, and especially due to the excess of theories and false news about current situations, just one year after the start of this war. I cannot imagine the impotence of the relatives of people who died from this virus, of not being able to be with them in the last moments, and not only that, but when they entered a hospital they did not know if they were their last moments.

Night was falling when Juanito entered the studio, where I was performing some work, still confused by the tragic news.

— Dad, what if I don't connect to class tomorrow and we camp in the garden.

Juanito's proposal was too tempting, especially knowing that every minute he studied was one less than the time I spent with him and added to the fact that not only cancer was the only danger to my life, but also the pandemic, insecurity in the city and economic and social crisis. Survival was becoming mission impossible. Therefore, the answer should not be complicated.

— Sure, son, and we took the opportunity to plant the little plant that your aunt gave us.

The next morning was perfect, despite not connecting to classes, Juanito woke up early to set up the tent and put it in the garden. We ask for some things to grill and be able to enjoy the little nature available inside our house.

When evening fell and we could still appreciate the sun's rays over the sea in the distance, we made a small fire imagining that we were in the Grand Canyon, a place that Juanito could barely remember because we were there when he was very little.

— Can we go as soon as you can travel? - He asked me again.

And for my part, I felt sad every time I had to lie to him for not causing him pain.

— Of course we will, son, don't worry about that. — I replied with a pat on the shoulder trying to give him the unconditional security that a child should receive from his father.

— Dad, and if I had been a woman, you would love me just the same. — He suddenly released. His questioning made me laugh out loud, just as the cool wind of that autumn night was blowing the tent from side to side.

— We knew you were a boy until the day you were born. — I replied. — Your mother and I didn't want to know before because we didn't really care, we just wanted to meet you and do it the old—fashioned way when there was no way to know the sex of a baby. So you can be sure of that: a son is the most important thing for a father regardless of his sex, character, beliefs, even if you were a fan of the Rayados of Monterrey my love for you would not vary one iota.

Juanito smiled when he heard the name of his favorite team that, although we have the same passion for soccer, respected him and supported his sympathy with a team different from mine.

It was done at dawn while we talked inside the tent, eating fried foods and drinking "Dr. Pepper ", the drink that fascinated us. It was then that I believed it was the right time to deliver a gift bought a week earlier, after an incessant search for few stores open due to the pandemic. It was a blue hardcover notebook to which I had pasted a legend that read: "Daddy's Teachings."

— Wait a minute, I'm going for a surprise that I have — I said and he just nodded, as I went to the living room of the house and extracted his gift from a drawer in the main display case.

— What's that, dad? A notebook for school! No, then, what a splendid gift, I didn't expect so much from you. - His sarcastic tone made me burst out laughing.

— No, son, it is a book where you will write the teachings that I want to leave you in case one day I miss.

— But you will never be absent dad, you will always be here with me.

7

Reunion

I saw her descend the stairs of that old restaurant, where we used to dine on weekends, and my heart felt the same emotion, as when I saw her smile for the first time. There we spent long hours drinking wine and talking about much nonsense: politics, religion, economics, and soccer; any subject was pleasant, as long as it came from her lips. Her gait was enigmatic; her transparent, beautiful gaze; but her smile, indescribable; it radiated magic; everything around lit up when she smiled. Always elegantly dressed, with her unparalleled demeanor, wearing black or dark blue.

People who appreciate me, both family and friends, hated her for what she did to me, and they urged me to do the same. For my part, I just couldn't hate her. She only made a mistake in her life and did not have to crucify her for that. Coldly analyzing the situation, perhaps her mistake was me and not him. I didn't fit in as much in her life, and although there was a great understanding between us, I was not the type of person she had always dreamed of. Probably her unconscious tried to make up for that fault with someone with whom she did share what she did not share with me. No one in my family spoke to her and I would have been the last person in the world who they thought would. However, she was legally and naturally the right person to care for and train Juanito for years to come.

Nobody better than a mother to take care of a child, despite our problems and how difficult the situation would be. It was to be expected, she imagined a thousand things about the matter of our meeting, and obviously they would all be bad, because she would be strange my urgency to see her to supposedly give her good news.

Despite that, it was incomprehensible to me because I had never complained about or wished for something bad, but from the tone of her voice, when she agreed to see us, I realized that she was predisposed not to have good news, and in fact they were not, but not they had nothing to do with any fault of her, on the contrary, she was part of the solution.

Her face showed more annoyance, the closer she got to the back table, where we always leaned against the wall, exhausted from drinking and talking. Now the situation did not imply a celebration, but it was also something delicate and I could only think of having a bottle on ice waiting for her, from whom I had drunk a glass to have the courage to tell her, bluntly what was happening. She was not quite settling into the chair, when with a signal I offered her a drink, but she shook her head in disapproval.

— Well, what do I owe this entertaining evening? — She said with a sarcasm that hurt me, but nevertheless I understood that she was doing it because she did not know the situation I was facing. I was sure that the moment I revealed the reason, her attitude would change. Meanwhile, her face was frowning more every second, especially when I asked the waiter for the menu. She did not want to order anything and her fiery gaze, although beautiful, forced me to hurry.

So she had to calm her aggressive attitude towards me, trying to get straight to the point and telling her the importance of our meeting. I took a large sip from the glass full of red wine until it was almost empty.

— I'm going to die! — I released it mercilessly, precisely when she turned to all sides so as not to meet her gaze with mine, trying to be indifferent. Instantly she stared at me with the intensity that always intimidated my pupils. Her jaw began to tremble slowly and her eyes danced more and more with tears. If my words hurt her, I was hopeless and seeing her suffers for me, I became uncontrollable crying.

Surely the subject of our meeting never crossed her mind, almost a year without seeing us; perhaps when she saw the bottle of wine she even thought of an attempt to win her back on my part, which I would gladly do, since she was the woman of my life. Maybe she thought of some nasty legal matter between us, one of those cumbersome and obnoxious ones. She was of delicate hands, with thin and soft fingers that liked to caress my cheeks every day, every hour, in our minutes. Now she was extending her arm, glass in hand, as if to pour her some wine. As an automaton I obeyed her. My hand was shaking holding the bottle. We couldn't say a single word.

How was it that from living together and sharing everything, we became in recent years the most bitter enemies. And now, with just four words, the harshest anger had softened. I gave her a smile as I lifted my glass of wine to her to wait for the answer. She tried to smile too, but her face wrinkled again. And then I released some of my spontaneous ones, which were the ones that she fell in love with at the time.

— Do I have to die for you to smile at me? — I told.

What a contrasting moment that joke made us laugh out loud and at the same time sob with tears; We didn't stop doing both, while we looked around, how the few people in the place looked at us strangely. At last, we only drank for a few minutes. We observe the beautiful view of the sea, shining a radiant blue from the intense rays of the sun. We laughed a little more, sobbing less and less and when each heart began to calm down, we were able to talk.

The next question was always the one that shortened the path to any redundancy the most.

— How long? — She asked in a shy voice, it was far from the fierce and atrocious sound on the other side of the receiver when I mentioned her. Now she was trying to be the most sensitive with me. I took a breath of air until it flooded my lungs and I felt like my body was still strong and getting stronger with each breath, and despite my tragedy, I touched my chin with my left hand and sighed.

— Two months — I managed to say.

Her cheeks, already reddened, were flooded with tears again; She tried to drink some water, but she could barely drink it.

— How can I help you? — She told me immediately. I was tempted to tell her that, nothing to me, but then Juanito was part of me, so she should help me a lot.

— You are legally the person with the right to take care of Juanito, in case you accept, otherwise you can allow my mother to take care of him — I released it without restriction. I was hoping that he would refuse, since it was surely not in his plans to take over our offspring, so that my mother could do it.

— Of course, I will take care of him and strive every day to become as important as you have been in his life. — She told me emphatically.

Her attitude was the opposite of expected. I gave me immense tranquility. At that moment I felt calm knowing that Juanito would not be alone, but that he would have a mother, the best he could have. I handed him my glass again to toast.

— Thank you! — I said. She stared at me and questioned me seriously:

— Why did you think I would refuse?

— I didn't think about it, it was just not to compromise you.

— Yes, you thought about it, do you think it was nice to get away from him, which is the most important thing for me? Product of love with the man I love the most in life.

Her statements stunned me and immediately my body began to sweat cold. My eyes locked on her pupils and I felt foolish for a moment, but I had to know the whole truth before I left.

— If I was so important in your life, why did you leave me? — was the question that came out in a reactionary way. I couldn't take that doubt to my grave after hearing that statement. For an instant she was silent; I noticed her too nervous and uncomfortable, which made me think it was just a phrase to make me feel good.

— And you still ask? — She returned another question, and I felt an idiot, but even more so for not understanding her answer.

It was like passing the problem to me; I was tempted to just close the conversation and leave the place, get away from her forever before losing my heart again, but she continued:

— Why did I fail you? - Her reddened face was filling with tears again. — How could I be with you again when I had been with someone else? I felt disappointed even in myself and that's why I decided to get away from the one person who has always loved me and shown that he would do everything for me.

After hearing those words, I felt a peace like never before since the day he left us.

— I would have forgiven you for anything, unless you left me and got away from us: we were a family — I said as a claim, but very subtly, using a very soft tone of voice.

And to top it all, our song began to be heard in the ambient sound, the waltz of our wedding. It was "She let you in her House", a song by Bruce Springsteen, soundtrack of the romantic movie "Secret Garden".

— Our song, — she said sobbing. — But you can forgive me now; I also suffered from not seeing you every day. Nobody has taken care of me like you; nobody gets up every morning and serves me a coffee in exchange for a kiss, forced if necessary. Nobody makes me laugh when I wake up and brightens my days even when my mood is the worst in the world. Nobody wakes me up at night, one minute before my birthday, and plays a joke on me just to wait for twelve o'clock. No one will earn you that right, that for years you claimed, to be the first to congratulate me. Nobody hides me when I did something wrong so as not to make me feel infamous. No—one like you.

I got up and hugged her very tightly, as you do with a loved one. Not in a romantic way, but brotherly, for what could have been the rest of our lives together.

I could go away in peace: I was the happiest man in the world at that moment; maybe I was also partly to blame because I shouldn't have let her go for the world, she was my wife and I should have tried to stop her in every possible way, bravely defend the home we had in the face of any adversity, and I just didn't do it, I just sat down to cry every day for her, to see how a wall was being built between the two of us, which only the circumstances of my departure broke down. Now each of us had a life made, an

excellent and happy life, not perfect as it was together, but it was
what we both had gained by not fighting for our own, when all this
time we should have been infinitely happy.

8

Christmas Eve

— Son, what would be your best Christmas present?

I had prepared myself for this question several days before, thinking about all the options that Juanito on occasion mentioned: a trip with his cousins to all the Disney parks, as happened on several of his birthdays; a large highway with remote control cars; one or more consoles to play video games, to which he was a regular; any sophisticated equipment for online entertainment, comfortably seated in a chair with virtual reality, or anything unthinkable for someone of my generation; perhaps the newest iPhone, the cost of which was higher than my computer. Any of these options represented a considerable investment.

It was not a common gift; however, there would not be another Christmas for another present, so it did not matter at that moment what his request was: I was prepared to pay for it. My life savings, it no longer made sense to keep saving them, when every second became a year for me.

Juanito looked at me like he had never done before: he was excited. He hugged me smiling and his words were the least expected, however, the most desired by me and by any parent at all times.

— My best gift? — He wondered.

For the first time he did not pounce urging an expensive gift, seen on the internet, on the contrary, his voice was serious and sincere, even his eyes shone a little as if wanting to cry.

He seemed to have ceased to be the mischievous child, with material desires to feel happy.

But what really took me by surprise was what he said right away:

— My best gift, dad, would be for you to spend all the Christmases of my life with me!

I heard his voice a little breathy and lower than usual. He had forgotten that he was a teenager about to turn 13.

His response shook me and a thousand memories passed through my mind together. From birth with her face swollen and reddish from childbirth; his first day of school in the yellow uniform, which was a little too big for him; his baptism, with a white robe that looked angelic to him; his first steps on the carpet in the house after some stumbling; the first time he yelled "papa", on a spring afternoon watching the horizon in the sea; his first soccer game, where the first ball he touched was an own goal, but we never touched on that subject again to overcome that obstacle in his mind and only think about positive things; his first choral declamation at the school flag swearing on the Monday after Father's Day, made me cry in front of all the parents; his first drawings, where his mother and I appeared in a house or in the country with bodies of different dimensions; his first birthday letters written to me, which I kept in the bottom drawer of my desk. I spent until the future moments imagining that I would be with him, graduating from the university with his toga and looking at me happily; or marry a beautiful woman just as tall as him, while sitting in church I thank God for that moment; or spending his first salary in a bar and telling me about his first job; or remind him after the age of forty, as a good father, that every six months he should have a prostate exam to prevent, advice that surely my father would have given me if he were still alive.

I couldn't hold back crying for long, so I hugged him very tightly and whispered in his ear, before my voice was cut off by tears:

—I will always be with you, Every Christmas, every day of your life ...

I immediately released him quickly and pretended I had to urgently go to the bathroom.

Inside those white mosaic walls I put on music and burst into the saddest and joyful cry of my life. Happy for the beautiful words just spoken by Juanito, but sadder also because I knew that I could not fulfill his request. I couldn't even vent my pain by hitting the objects in the bathroom with all my might, because he would notice and start to ask; however, hearing his words generated the strongest conflicting emotions of my life. On the one hand, I felt that I could die in peace: my memory in his mind would shine and would be remembered despite not having been in the most important moments of his life. On the other hand, it shattered me deep inside, knowing how much he wanted to spend the next Christmases of his life with me, when I could no longer do so. It was like having the world at my feet, when I no longer had time to enjoy it, and I felt immense frustration.

— Dad, are you okay? — He asked me as he knocked on the bathroom door.

Try as I might, I couldn't hold back crying, so I tried to excuse my cracking voice for an upset stomach.

— Yes, son, you know: those tacos that we ate in the morning made me a little heavy — I told him convincingly, and immediately I could hear his boat laugh soon.

— Dad, but if you have a stomach of steel: you can eat stones and nothing happens to you — he joked, and that made me feel better, despite the convulsions of feelings that I was experiencing at that time from laughing out loud.

— I'm old now, son. Turn on the TV that the San Francisco 49ers game is going to begin. Right now I'm ordering your favorite pizza so we can see it.

Every Sunday, Juanito would watch American football with me, although I'm sure he didn't understand anything about that sport, but we enjoyed eating all kinds of sweets.

— You're great, dad, thank you; Can I get you a beer? — He said between laughter and doubt about my state of health.

— Yes, please — I managed to say excited by the detail of watching the game with me, when I knew beforehand he didn't like it — with a beer the discomfort will surely go away.

9

Last Christmas Eve

The disease was beginning to wreak havoc on me: I was getting up long after the first roosters and in unmerciful and perennial pain. Juanito came up to me during his online class break and made a very nice proposal, even though I didn't feel like it at all. He told me to order something from McDonald's for lunch.

— Dad, imagine you're at the McDonald's at the Arc de Triomphe in Paris, where you didn't know how to order because everything was automated and in French.

Marketers should study this success story, not like a franchise that sells a hamburger.

Nobody with two fingers of head would eat a hamburger in the most beautiful place in the world, with the Champs Elysses in the background. I still remember the shame of entering that place and leaving with nothing in hand for not knowing how to use technology.

McDonald's, according to my point of view and seeing the emotion of my son when he asked me for food from that place, had achieved generations of happy children, not satisfied, simply happy, because they saw the adults still enjoy attending this place. For my part, I was almost certain it was there, not because of the obnoxious taste, but because of the feeling of happiness to remember the happiest moments of my childhood and the McDonald's souvenirs. However, I felt very bad that day and just wanted to disappear from the face of the earth. It lifted my spirits a bit to have breakfast from that place on our last December 24 together. No one can imagine the pain caused by this terrible terminal illness.

Long ago it had become, not only the suffering of the century, but an incurable evil. Juanito wanted me to go get his breakfast and I barely had the strength in my fingers. I just wanted to ease the pain, but I saw him tender, unique smile and I better dried my tears.

— What's the matter, dad? — He asked me worried.

— Nothing, son, I think something spicy got into my eye. — I said and immediately went to get our breakfast as quickly as possible to return quickly and enjoy one more moment with him.

We stayed like this for a long time, slowly enjoying the food and even more so when the last two classes had been suspended because the torrential rain damaged the electricity supply in the teachers' home. That's why we enjoy the scenery of the Champs—Elysées, and then we walk slowly to the Arc de Triomphe.

What at first had become exhausting by disinfecting all the packages or packages that came from outside; clean even soda containers, rinse coins with soap and wash hands for twenty seconds, inspired by the technique that cooks use to ensure a lower probability of letting that virus into the house. The room was converted into an excellent enclosure to prevent all kinds of diseases and that also contributed to not having as many episodes as that day, of feeling that the pain was killing me.

Shortly after, we started getting our clothes ready for that date and making the final arrangements for the dinner our little family would host at home. We decided to release a suit that we had bought a vacation before for that occasion. They were two sacks in gray tones that gave us a modern, but formal touch. The table was for six people: my mother, my sister, her daughter Fernanda,

Juanito and me. My mother instilled in us that the empty place was for the Christ Child who was born that night. Fortunately, a day before, we had had the help of everyone involved to decorate the house with the Christmas theme. It helped a lot to have a beautiful fireplace built at the request of Juanito's mother to spend long hours sitting drinking coffee. There we hang Christmas colored socks and decorate every corner. The atmosphere even felt a bit chilly, in a city where, although the temperature drops a bit in December, it doesn't stop feeling hot.

We had some gifts for each of our guests, but the main thing was to be together and taste the delicacies prepared by each of the attendees: Juanito made a pineapple dessert known as carlota, which was my favorite; I prepared cod, because I loved it and I also thought that in a coastal place you could not miss a seafood on the table. My mother cooked a pork leg and my sister, turkey. My niece Fernanda would make her specialty: chocolate brownies that, although that flavor was not to my satisfaction, they looked so delicious that I devoured the one they served me in no time.

At eleven o'clock at night we started dinner, but not before praying for food and for a closer Christmas together. Nobody assumed that for me it was the last. With five minutes to twelve, we made a prayer holding hands. It fascinated me to be like this, as a family, on a date to reflect. My thoughts were positive, I had an excellent family and I was making a great man in Juanito. I didn't have to worry about anything, however, with each passing day, each hour, each second, my heart raced thinking about the end.

The Christmas hug, right at midnight, was too emotional that I could not contain the tears, fortunately with some medicines taken at noon, the discomfort that started in the morning had already passed. It was a big hug for my mother, who also cried, because, like my sister, she knew of my early departure. With my sister the hug was also a bit sad. My niece was the one who raised a smile at me, since I played board games with her every Christmas, and finally I hugged Juanito tightly, for a long time and every second I asked God to grant him health and wisdom.

After the sentimental episode, we went to the room where we would open the gifts. Each had four present, one from each family member gathered that night. I gave my mother a beautiful painting that I got from an art gallery. It was the painting of a mother and a son walking on the sand of the beach, an excellent excuse for her to always remember me in her living room. I gave my sister a bracelet that represented our brotherhood. I gave my niece the bag she wanted so much and for which she had been saving for months. I gave Juanito the video game console that he had asked me to continue enjoying what he most wanted at his age. What would become of him when he grew up? Would he drink beer with his friends at the beach as I did? How many children would he have? What name would he give them? All these questions flooded my mind when my niece interrupted me:

— Uncle, it's your turn to make the toast.

I was sure that Fernanda's desire was more to taste the sparkling wine than to listen to me. I had no idea what to say. I could not in a minute summarize everything that was inside.

— I, just ... — I started a little nervous —. I rather wish that this Christmas the love that God has given us for this date will be born in our hearts, since the most important thing is the love of our family members and we must feel fortunate to have the time that God gives us to do so and I hope that we always remember this Christmas, and even though many years pass, we always return to this place to realize the only important thing in our lives.

They gave us five in the morning playing card guessing. I didn't want it to end that Christmas Eve.

10

Last days

There were just three days left until the end of the year and therefore also my existence. I knew beforehand that he could survive a few more days, weeks, maybe months, but it wouldn't be the same anymore. Instead of transcending as a hero for Juanito it would be a very heavy burden in his short life. Something complicated and painful was coming to delegate to a 12—year—old. I couldn't stop running for more minutes, so as soon as I woke up.

I decided to resume our unfinished task a month ago. I went to the bookcase in his room full of video game stickers and colored pencils. I took out a blue hardcover notebook with the legend

— The lessons of dad. — There was not much time left and he had to capture useful advice there for his life, and that it was a guide and also an instrument to get closer when I was gone. — It's time to write down, son. — I said, showing him the notebook. He smiled and took a pen from the dining room desk and sat down ready to write everything down.

— This will be the time to do this every day? — He asked me. I hadn't thought of it that way, but it was a good alternative to get into the habit in the few days that I had left.

— Yes, well, although I can also remember some teaching at any time of the day and tell you to write it down so I don't forget it.

— Perfect, Dad. — He told me, and I was wondering how to begin to dictate my experiences of daily life.

And I started with what I considered the most important: filling the house with decorations during the Christmas season, evoking the birth of the Child God.

— The first will be: always have faith in God and in yourself. That will lead you to achieve everything you set your mind to, son. — I expressed serious and sure.

— Excellent, dad, I will always follow your advice, — he said decidedly. — What would number two be?

To that question, the first image that crossed my mind was that of my father at the age of 14 teaching me to tie my tie to attend my first quinceañera party, of a classmate of my older sister. From that moment to date, hundreds of events have passed: fifteen years, graduations, book burning, weddings, and I never forgot those moments, nor did I forget the talent to tie that symmetrical double loop knot, not the lazy one that many make young, only one turn and looks like a deformed triangle on the neck.

Coincidentally, that night, we had decided to record his first video as a "youtuber", to recommend video games to other children with the same hobby. So I had the ideal pretext to dress him in a tie and start my second item on the list of things I wanted to inherit from him. Although in this case we could reinforce it, not only with the written explanation, but also with a video.

— But, Dad, how am I going to wear a tie: no "gamer" wears it, we hardly worry about fixing ourselves and less right now with the pandemic!

I loved his reproaches, with his angelic face. It was then that I remembered my father's wise words and used them as an argument.

— Do you want to be like the rest? Don't you want to look better to differentiate yourself and start having your own audience?

Although the argument was not very convincing in a 12—year—old boy, he accepted more out of parental authority than being convinced. I was proud to see him standing upright, with an immense stature, a couple of centimeters to match my meager five feet. I imagined him in a couple of years, already without me, made an oak, playing basketball and plunging the ball into the hoop without straining, or playing football, tackling opponents for the yards of the field, or in soccer, jumping to finish with head above all opponents. He learned how to tie the knot quickly, with a couple of explanations. Right away I saw him making his first video and I was proud to witness such an important event in his life.

When I finished recording, I asked him to sit down again so he could take the blue notebook and write down one more lesson of the day.

— Ready, tell me, dad.

— Treat others as you want them to treat you.

— I like that teaching, Dad, although in school sometimes there are children who annoy others.

— They probably didn't have a father to teach them that, son.

— Are we finished for today?

— No, write down, the greatest happiness for a father is to see or hear the smile of a son.

— Yeah, dad, really!

— I'm serious, son, nothing makes me happier than when you're happy. That has been my greatest happiness in life.

— Thanks Dad. Can we continue watching series?

— Well, but just let me dictate one more and that's it.

— Okay, but just one more, my hand hurts from so much writing.

— Do not be exaggerated, and note: God has shared his power to create the universe through the power of the mind, and that is why we must always think positively to create everything we want.

— That is true?

— Of course it's true, son.

— So, can I create whatever I want?

— Everything you wish.

11

Last day of my last year: 2020

It was always my favorite date of the year. One more return from the Earth to the Sun. The ideal moment to reflect, toasts the victories, forget the defeats and give infinite thanks for being alive one more year.

Although Christmas had already passed, the atmosphere is still flooded by that spirit of harmony. By then my life expectancy was two months, but it was already 67 days. And I was grateful to God for having reached this moment, with great force, and that made me think that I could survive another month.

I had woken up almost at dawn, and I went out for a run on the shore of the beach. I wanted to purify my lungs, with the morning breeze, and then my soul watching the sunrise on the horizon of the sea. Then I came home and made coffee. I started to bake some "waffles" so that when I told Juanito what I had cooked he would get up immediately. That's what he did when I prepared something tasty for him and he had to take classes. He would wake up motivated to enjoy something tasty before his classes.

It was almost ten o'clock in the morning and Juanito still did not give any indication of getting up and the truth was he did not intend to truncate his dream. So I thought about what I could do in the meantime to make the most of my last day with him. I had forgotten something important, to write him a goodbye letter to read a few days after learning the truth. So I sat on the bureau, in front of his bed, and began to write, watching him rest deeply. He gave me just enough time, since when he opened his slanted eyes from so much sleep, I was finishing the letter ending with "Your dad loves you."

— What are we going to have for breakfast, dad?

— Whatever you want, son; Choose from the options to order at home at once, so that at the end we can review the details of today's dinner.

— Perfect, I want pizza.

— Piiiiizza ?! At this time?

— Well, you didn't tell me what I wanted!

— Yes, you're right, son, we'll both eat pizza.

Right away, I grabbed the metal ad stuck on the refrigerator for his favorite franchise. And I ordered the long—awaited pizza, which arrived right away. After devouring all the slices of the four—cheese pasta, we began to prepare the perfect night. We were going to say goodbye to what many had called an atypical, unwanted, terrible year; however, it was one more year of life. We start with the grapes: we separate five glasses with twelve grapes each and store them in the refrigerator ready to add a little cider at night.

Every tick of the clock's second hand was like silver bullets entering my heart. I knew that each beat of the clock was one second less of my existence. I had predicted a sad and painful day, but it was meaning the opposite. I was happy for all the moments lived, for being at peace with the world, knowing that even without me the people I loved the most would be immensely happy.

Juanito and I arranged the suitcases in the living room for the moment of the ritual of going out with them on our shoulders to the street to attract the good vibes. Again the feeling came to me imagining the trips we would not do, but his sense of humor gave me peace of mind.

— Excellent, dad. And this year with the pandemic, where will we travel? To the cakes nearby or the tacos by the boardwalk?

— Nothing is impossible, son, you just have to have faith and you will see that you will travel wherever you want this 2021.

— I will travel? We will travel, dad, but who will bore me with their boring explanations and stories of each place visited.

There would be no "we will travel", but I was pleased to know that when I was somewhere I would remember those "boring explanations".

— Of course, you will never get rid of me; What's more, when you get married, I'll go live in your house, with you and your wife.

— Dad, what things do you say! I'm hardly a teenager to be thinking about that.

We set the table for the five people who would be there, just like on Christmas Eve. The joke was to do everything together to spend every second of my last day of life with him.

As my mother and sister knew the outcome of this story, they agreed to arrive in the afternoon so that they could all live together as a family and celebrate the New Year.

The day before we performed the traditional "old man", this represented a beautiful traditional family. Some sewed each hole in the clothing consisting of pants and a shirt as large as possible, to prevent the materials placed inside from coming out of the doll. Others were filling it with explosives and newspaper that had the effect of keeping the fire alive in order to ignite all the powder from each small rocket. Others designed the face, sometimes we used a mask of a famous person who died that year, or some new design or even sometimes it was just a face drawn with a down on the fabric of a shirt that formed the head. While the adults enjoyed good music and wine, and the children sweets and soft drinks, always with the illusion that each year the decibels of the explosion were stronger, which represented a great year lived. More than a tradition of the city it was a family cult, like a ritual inherited by generations from the grandparents; perhaps it was one of the few traditions that could be maintained, despite the passing of the years; some said that it was part of the Totonaca culture, but here also centuries before were the Olmecs, and probably even the Mayans. For sure it was not known, if it was inherited from any of these cultures or a mixture of all to celebrate one more return from the Earth to the Sun. It was like a way of saying goodbye to the experiences of the year, and how it had been a difficult year. We did with the most wanted desire to forget about 2020. Perhaps this custom would be one of the things they would miss the most, in theory, because they did not know where people go when they die. Nobody knew it, nobody scientifically could assure it. That at times was my biggest fear, but I always tried to think that it couldn't be something unpleasant, on the contrary, being a believer forced me to think about a better life; That is why, at my death, I imagined observing and caring for them from some imperceptible place, another dimension, the sky, limbo, the ether, an alternate space, or wherever it was. Given the unfortunate events of the year, on the sign carried by that doll full of newspaper and explosives, it had a simple but profound phrase: "go now, 2020." I laughed every time I watched him, at the irony of the message.

They all arrived on time for coffee and some tea, accompanied by fritters, my mother's specialty. We talked about all the experiences of the year, from the beginning when we could still freely go out onto the streets, without mouth covers, and attend massive events.

Nobody imagined that the start of our 2020, which had started with family trips, trips to the movies, would be upset in the third month.

And much less do we imagine that this serious world situation would last so long, even on that last day of the year we did not know when we would return to our normal activities. The new normal forced us to live in fear, locked up, away from the world. Yet we had ourselves.

After having fun with all kinds of board games and laughing out loud for hours, we sat down at the table at eight at night. It was very early to do it, however, it was also a ritual and above all it should be a relaxed moment, enjoying it, without rushing. We began to taste some dishes as an appetizer, while we filled our glasses with cider and each one made a toast. My mother and my sister toasted to be together for another year, trying to avoid crying so that Juanito would not realize the reality.

— I toast because this year my dad has a more relaxed character. — Juanito said. And I just smiled and nodded. In fact, I would no longer have to deal with my scolding.

— I toast for my uncle — Fernanda commented and for a moment I thought she was saying it to upset Juanito, but no, her face changed too much and a couple of tears ran down her cheeks — because he is always with us, every year, in every moment, every Christmas dinner, in the New Year's toast, from wherever, but always close to us.

At that moment, my mother got up to get the turkey for dinner. She couldn't help the tears. I turned to see my sister, with a frown, in protest for having told Fernanda the truth, but she also burst into tears. So, I had to try to make them forget to think about my death in that moment of happiness.

— This is how it will be: no doubt, but hey, I toast for a year full of success for you and all of us who are here, but above all with perfect health. That should fill us with optimism and happiness, so there is no reason to be sad. Nor that the Red Sharks of Veracruz had lost and descended again.

Everyone smiled at the comment and I managed to relax the moment.

It was approaching midnight and we took the "old man" to the sidewalk to place him on a metal chair, away from any house where any spark from the explosions could reach. We set up a table outside the house, with the glasses and the grapes. Everything was ready to say goodbye to 2020.

With five minutes to go until midnight, we lit the "old man" with a little gasoline and in a few seconds the explosions began to sound repeatedly, while we lit sparklers to make way for the grapes, just as the church bells rang. I hugged my mother very hard, as well as my sister and then Juanito.

— May this year be the best for you, Dad. — Juanito told me in the New Year's hug.

— So be it, son, God willing.

Fernanda gave me a big hug and whispered in my ear:

— We're going to miss you a lot, uncle.

— I know, Fer, I will also do it, how, when and where, I don't know, but I'm sure I will.

And before bursting into tears, I invited Fer to take her suitcase. So we walked around the block dragging a suitcase, according to us to attract luck to travel all year round, and to distant lands.

It was the "old man" that took the longest to fade in our family history. We all smiled, hugged, drank cider, turned on some lights, gazed at the stars on a cool night, and a beautiful moon welcoming

2021. We entered the house and sat in the living room to write down each of our purposes for the 2021.

— What are your New Year's resolutions? — Juanito asked me.

— Being very close to all of you. — I replied.

We laughed and celebrated all night, until one by one we were overcome by sleep, and it was time to say goodbye. The clock read half past five in the morning and by seven he should be at the airport. They all knew them, so they gave me a big hug, before leaving, as we promised: we should all be smiling, even if it was a difficult moment. From carrying Juanito, from the living room to his bedroom, my back started to hurt, but it would probably be the last time it happened to me, so I enjoyed it, although I could barely straighten myself from the pain. I packed the last things in my suitcase while I waited for six thirty in the morning and the taxi I had ordered passed me by.

I heard him arrive and I approached him for the last time to say in his ear:

— I love you, son, take good care of yourself.

Juanito was completely asleep, but even so he managed to hear me and had the strength to whisper to me:

— Thanks Dad.

12

The letter

"With you I have lived the twelve most beautiful years of my life: you are the person I have loved the most in the world. You probably think it's a few years, I also think so, however, they were spectacular. I have no idea where I'll go, but I'm sure I'll know about you wherever I am. I have infinite faith that it will.

There is no more difficult situation in life than writing a posthumous letter for the person you love the most in life. I will think that you are sitting in front of me, talking to you about my concerns, before leaving.

The first thing I want you to do with my inheritance, the product of my life's work, when you are 18 years old, is to travel to Florence. It is the most beautiful place I have ever known. If you look at the cathedral, from the door to its foundations, it is a work of art, different from all existing ones, with green, white and pink colors that give it a unique touch and look incredible. I want you to arrive at sunset and sit in any open bar around. Ask for a bottle of wine, with two glasses, like when I did it with my father on some occasion. I'll be there with you toasting your happiness. It will be incredible, as it was for me, to see that beautiful work of art accompanied by the best drink in the world and my dearest person in the world.

I also want that every evening in our city you walk towards the sea, see the sunset full of beautiful nuances, because there I was inspired to write some of the stories that I will leave archived on my computer, for you to read and publish. But the best story was always to see you being born, growing up and I hope to observe you from somewhere becoming a good and happy man.

I have left you my collection of chess boards, collected since I was a child. Take great care of the 49ers against Dallas, and I only recommend always choosing the pieces of the Niners, your father's favorite team. Maybe there we will win.

On my shelf I keep a turquoise blue polo shirt. It is the memory of the first time I kissed your mother. If it hadn't been for that Halloween night, maybe you would have different parents, more consenting, less dramatic. I don't know, but they wouldn't love you more than me.

I still have the newspaper from February 23, 2008, when you were born. I leave it on my desk for you to read and realize how different the world was a decade ago. Do you want to know how I found out about you? It is one of those moments that are never forgotten: I had been arriving from Havana, where I was studying for my doctorate. I was tired, overwhelmed by a thousand details that I had to correct in my doctoral thesis. Suddenly, my cell phone rang, and it was your mother, with some magic words: 'we are having a baby'. Right away I imagined a thousand crazy things: us in the stadium singing and jumping with joy next to the 'barras bravas' of our city's soccer team. Accompanying you in the serenade to your girlfriend. Taking you to your first day of college, obviously to my alma mater, Sotavento University. Cheering at your soccer, baseball, basketball or American games. I imagined your hobbyist number. All that passed through my mind, soon after, barely aware of your birth.

I also ask you to stay at home every 29th of May. It may be my suggestion, but I always thought that that day was bad luck for the family, because precisely on those dates of different years my maternal grandparents passed away.

When you meet the woman that you consider will accompany you the rest of your life, take her to the place where your mother and I were happy, to the beach where one day she took me and said that nothing would separate us, even though she knew about the 'earthquake' that was coming to our relationship.

I confess: I was left with the enormous desire to meet Mount Everest. I hope that you do manage to live that experience. I don't expect you to climb it, because that requires a lot of preparation, but I do expect you to get there to contemplate its majesty, that you can have a few beers and feel like a lucky man to meet it, like when we reached the top of the Great Wall of China. You remember? Your cheeks were too red, burned from the intense cold. You were sweating down the hundreds of steps up. When we stepped onto the last step, I felt like I was reaching paradise, because of the feeling of victory, feeling relaxed because of the cold wind blowing on my face, but more than anything because it was an achievement together.

I could write you hundreds of sheets, but I will only use this time while you wake up from your deep sleep, on this our last day of living together.

I remember when you attended my soccer games. I was motivated to run more and give myself to the maximum, because I had to earn your admiration. Your smile in the stands made me happy, regardless of the outcome of the game. The best marker was your restless smile, waiting for me to come and greet you and enjoy a Sunday together, eating junk food and sweets.

I leave you as a legacy the books I wrote. Read them! And in a low voice, tell me if you liked them, that I'll be listening to you from heaven. I think my best novel is 'A perfect design', because it opened up the possibility, even if it is science fiction, of one day seeing you again, which is what I want the most right now.

I would like to be able to go back in time, like in my novel 'Yesterday', and do a thousand things with you. All the rights to those novels are yours, so you can do what you want, although I would like you to have the pleasure of writing and continue to increase the family library.

I tell you that when they told me, sitting in the coldness of an office, that it would be my last months of life, the first thing that came to mind was you, because you are the most important thing in my life.
Juanito, with you I always wanted to walk the route traveled by the protagonists of my novel 'Always you', from Madrid to La Coruña. Go through it and confirm if it is as fascinating as I wrote it, without knowing it, by pure imagination. Try the Galician octopus, to see if it is as delicious as the Galicians boast.

There are so many places in the world that I wish you knew about for me, like Old Trafford, where Manchester United plays. That city has the ingredients that fascinate me: soccer, beer and alternative music.

I left you on the video player the 24 Hour Party People movie, where it makes a remembrance of the day when the punk music movement began to take shape in the world, just on June 4, 1976 (the day your father was born) in a Sex Pistols concert, where there were only 42 attendees, among them were the members of the Warsaw group, which would later become Joy Division, and with the suicide of its vocalist it would change its name to New Order, my favorite group. There were also the members of the group Buzzcocks and Mick Hucknall, in that same place, before all of them were famous, in a coincidence that gave a whole style of music to the whole world, just as the boring Beatles did in Liverpool. I imagine you in a decade remembering me, on a mourning anniversary day or my birth, listening to New Order, drinking beer in a Manchester bar, with the song Ceremony, or perhaps listening to it in the same stadium.

I remember when I was in Milan, at the San Ciro stadium, and at the end of the game I carried an immense teddy bear, with the red and black team shirt, until I returned to Bergamo, where I gave a conference entitled 'Right to education'. In the vicinity of the stadium, on the bus, on the train, in the taxi, everyone stared at me, teasingly and curiously, but I was excited with my big bear.

Never forget our trip to Buenos Aires, when you were barely six years old. We were dying of cold. You wore a red scarf and we walked hand in hand, together with your mother. We were walking the path that Borges followed to get to Beatriz Viterbo's house, in his famous tale of 'El Aleph'. You had no idea what we were doing when we took the train and went through various stations, while you were singing "I didn't stop the party." Every time I see that video of you singing, the emotion wins me over. Go back to that place, son, and drink a coffee as strong and hot as possible to counteract the cold, and walk on Alvear street, until you feel tired, that we have exhausted ourselves from walking so much and you must return, after imagining that point, from where you can see all the places in the universe, located in the basement of Beatriz Viterbo's house, does exist, and you can see me through it.

Finally, remember that before the pandemic broke out we went to the Mexican Tennis Open to fulfill one of your most cherished dreams: to see the best tennis player in the world, Rafa Nadal, play with his hammer racket and terrible balls that kept you speechless all the time.

It was an honor to have been your father these twelve years.
See you soon, gammer ".

13

On The Way

Dead alive from wanting to return and hug him again, I avoided turning to see the front door of the house. If I had, I would never have been able to say goodbye, so I went on my way. I got into the taxi driven by a man, whose face looked no more than forty years old.

He wore a red shirt representative of the soccer team of our city, "Los Tiburones Rojos de Veracruz."

— Is something wrong, sir? — The driver asked me worriedly.

— No, why do you ask? — I replied with a broken voice.

— You are very pale, and I don't know if you are in a hurry to get to the "Taurino Caamano Ramos" airport.

— No, I'm not in a rush. We have had a good time.

— Okay, if you need something you tell me.

— Yes, do not worry. I'm stressed out by various things, but it would be difficult to explain.

— Ok, I understand.

— Just take the entire path to the boardwalk, please.

In those moments I wanted to see the sunrise over the sea for the last time.

— Yes, sir, as you order.

There were only two ways to get to the airport: through the city and the other by the boulevard that runs along the coast. I never noticed a difference in distance or time. My whole life seemed to pass in slow motion, precisely when we began to walk along the boardwalk. I had thousands of anecdotes in every meter of that avenue. In it I celebrated many "Christmas Eve" and "old years" watching the new dawn, as it was happening now, but at that moment I was sober and depressed. Little by little the journey was getting shorter. We got to where the boulevard joins the avenue that would lead us towards the airport. Through the rear—view mirror I kept observing how little by little that blue color was disappearing, which I would never see again. Without that view, I came out of the trance in which it made me see that beautiful landscape.

— How is our team doing? — I asked the taxi driver, alluding to the red shirt he was wearing.

— Whoops! As always, very bad. We are the mockery every tournament. Last week, the Pumas scored eight goals for us — he told me in a resigned voice, but encouraged to start the conversation.

— I believe that Veracruz is a land of art, poetry, dance, music, but not a hotbed of athletes, bohemia wins us over.

— Well yes, but even so one always hopes that they win something. I hope one day we will see them be champions.

— Hopefully!

— You'll see, someday we will achieve it — the driver was excited defending his team that was precisely seventy years after winning the championship —. Can you imagine that day? The city would go crazy, it would be holidays day and night.

— Don't doubt that, — I also said excitedly, — you see that we are great for the party. That's why when the players come they don't give up; they fall into the temptation of this magical noisy city.

— Yes, it's a shame that that always happens. And what will you do when they win the championship? — The driver questioned me without taking his eyes off the road.

— I will go crazy with joy, I will go out to sing and shout on the boardwalk all day and night. I'll take my wife to dance salsa, while we get drunk with joy — I replied without any discomfort, knowing that I would not be alive when that happened, well, if they ever achieve the championship —. It's probably not here. I do not know when I returned to the city, but it will be a pleasure, from wherever I am, to celebrate the triumph of the team of my loves.

— Don't worry: here we will celebrate for you.

— That seems excellent to me, but I also wanted to see if you can do something more for me, in case that historic moment comes one day.

— Of course sir. If that moment comes, it will be fantastic. So you tell me what is offered to you.

— It's something a bit complex, but I hope, when the time comes, you can support me. My son lives in the residence where you picked me up. I would like that the day the Sharks become champions again, you bring him a small present.

— But what if championship never come out.

— I have faith that they will achieve it one day not too far away. How do you see? Could you do me that big favor? Obviously, it would be a well—paid service.

— Look, if they are champions, you do not need to pay me anything; I go, free of charge, to the door of your son's house and give him what you like.

— The complicated part of the matter is that I would need you to buy that present. — I clarified as I handed him a roll of thousand—peso bills, "and take it that same night."

— And what happens if I die before?

— Don't worry: I know what the risks are, and I don't mind losing that investment, but I need your help.

— Well, if you trust me, go ahead. Tell me what you want me to buy.

— Of course I trusted you: we Veracruz people have a word and we fully comply with our commitments.

— That without a doubt, sir.

— I want you to buy our team's shirt, with the number ten on the back and put the name of my son Juanito.

— Only that?

— Yes just that. I know it is a very big request, but you have no idea how I will thank you for that gesture towards me.

— Well, if God lends me life to see them win, you can be sure that your order will come.

14

Goodbye

December is the only time of the year when it feels a bit chilly in the city. With twenty—one degrees we are already taking out the sweaters. The lowest temperature I can remember is seventeen degrees, and we coastal people almost froze.

Here at the airport there is a colder climate: in the chairs, the handrails, the tables, in everything metallic. I stood in line to document with healthy distance; They took my temperature, filled out a health survey, and put gel on my hands on the threshold of the last waiting room. How I missed when we could breathe freely and everywhere. Hopefully, one day, those who remain on the planet can solve this problem, so that we can talk again with our own and strangers, without fear of contracting that microscopic enemy. Despite the pandemic situation, I felt lucky because, with my deteriorating health, having contracted the coronavirus, I probably couldn't even get to the inns. "Thank you, my God," I repeated every time I appreciated that.

I sat on one of the uncomfortable benches at the airports, and through the huge glass wall I could see the plane in which I would depart. As there was a decade since my departure, I no longer recognized any passengers. The city had grown exponentially and many of the young people sitting around it were probably children when I met their families, and so it was very difficult to recognize each other.

I ordered an espresso to wake me up and calm down. The further I got away; I felt my body begin to tremble with fear from the uncertainty of my destiny. I just took the first sip and felt how the taste of coffee ran down my throat until it reached my stomach and began to affect my eyes, which closed involuntarily, for not having slept. It was drizzling a little and with the low temperature the glass would be determined and I only saw blurred images of the other passengers. I had sat as close to the walls and looked out so that no one would notice my pain and because I did not want to talk to anyone.

I was beginning to feel a very deep depression, because I knew that I would never see any of my loved ones again. And that terrified me; it made me sweat, despite the cold increased by the air conditioning of the place. I inhaled the steam of the coffee trying to calm me down, with that aroma that I adored so much. On the loudspeaker they indicated that the flight was delayed twenty minutes and that gave me more chills, since the time was shortened.

A very elegant old woman, who must have been beautiful when she was young because all her features were perfect, approached me. She had a symmetrical nose, almost perfect; large, blue eyes; unmatched lashes and impeccably combed. Her lotion reminded me of the one my mother used, very soft, and like her, it generated great confidence in me. However, in those moments I didn't want to talk to anyone: I just wanted to be alone, at peace with me and suffer as little as possible in the remaining time on my calendar.

> — These flights are always delayed. - she said in an attempt to get me to talk, but I just nodded. And even though I didn't hold my gaze for two seconds, she questioned me again:

— Are you nervous about the flight?

On the one hand, I was about to be rude in my gestures with her, because I was not used to talking with strangers. And yet, I answered her politely again, only shaking my head from side to side, in denial and hoping this time to finish the conversation.

However, not only was I nervous, I was dying of fear, but I could not tell a stranger. The lady was not daunted by the attempt to snub and put her cold hand on mine, and in addition to the surprise I felt a hot energy, like when one is motivated to do what one likes the most.

— Fear blinds, faith grants. — she told me and immediately stood up to leave the place. Her words eventually imploded my mind. "Fear blinds, faith grants," it hammered at me for the next few minutes.

Suddenly, I heard a noise on the ceiling and turned to see the huge lamps that illuminated the incipient cloudy morning. They were blinking and soon all the airport lights went out. I just sat there waiting for the blackout to fix. I assumed there must be a light plant. At that moment I felt like running on the soft sand of the beach, inhaling the cool breeze, with endless energy. How could I feel like this if I was hopeless? I didn't understand it. The light returned a couple of minutes later. I kept looking at the wet glass, how the drops descended, making the view outwards translucent. I always liked looking at this effect. I had not paid attention to all the passengers in the room when I entered; however, after the blackout I had the perception that there were fewer people in the place. Out of nowhere, the elegant lady, of the world, appeared with another gesture of kindness:

— Calmer?

I didn't feel like talking to anyone, but, nevertheless, at that moment she felt friendlier, as an old acquaintance, as if I was talking to my grandmother, who was my adoration as a child, and she was always there to take care of me. She taught me to pray and from that moment my life was full of great moments, every time I used prayer as a solution to my problems.

— Yes — I said in a low voice.

— Who is that person you can trust the most? — She answered me still in an unexpected way.

— My father — I said while I did not understand why every word I crossed with her filled me with peace.

— So, if one day you had to take an unknown path, uncertain for you, if he were by your side, would you not feel fear?

The words of the unknown woman filled my eyes with tears that I could not contain, and I only managed to answer her laconically:

— No.

— Turn to your left side, on the last bench, can you see that passenger? — At that moment I could barely see through the tears, however, too much precision was not necessary at a great distance, since I could distinguish that person by his prominent hairline recesses very similar to mine. — Are you still feeling fear? No right? I think, then, you're ready to board.

The person on the last bench got up slowly, although paradoxically with a jovial walk that I could distinguish from all my life and with each step he took it was like when I felt sick as a child and I saw him approach to tell me that the condition would disappear. Or like when I fell off my bicycle as a teenager; lying in the street, bleeding from my foot and scared, I saw him coming and with every step he approached the pain and fear diminished. Or like when I was in a car accident and I was in shock; by chance he was passing by, and I felt absolute confidence that everything would be fine. Many years later, things had not changed: with each step he took to get closer, any iota of fear was disappearing. Now I was more certain than ever of the way forward, even though I didn't know it. In the darkest, most uncertain moment of my life, I was seeing the face of the person I trusted the most.

The beautiful old woman was slowly moving away from the place.

Meanwhile, I smiled when I began to see the face of the person who approached me. He had the usual smile, the usual one, like when he joked with me as a child, and he would laugh that laugh, and we were very happy.

I got up immediately and hugged him very hard, no longer crying and without feeling any fear; on the contrary, I wanted to go down that road with pleasure, even if I did not know the destination. He wouldn't stop smiling. I imagined that one day I would expect Juanito in the same way. In an instant the cloudy sky cleared and the sunlight became more radiant than ever.

     — It's time to go.

And we began to walk, without turning around; we just talked and advanced.

     — Where are we going, dad?

     — To the most beautiful place you can imagine.